Sometimes

Sometimes

Keith Baker

Green Light Readers
Harcourt Brace & Company
San Diego   New York   London

Printed in Hong Kong

Sometimes I am happy.

Sometimes I am sad.

I like who I am.

I like what I do.

Sometimes I am hot.

Sometimes I am cold.

I like who I am.

I like what I do.

Sometimes I am up.

Sometimes I am down.

I like who I am.

I like what I do.

Sometimes I am red.

Sometimes I am blue.

I'm all of these things.
What about you?

First Green Light Readers edition 1999
Green Light Readers is a trademark of Harcourt Brace & Company.

Library of Congress Cataloging-in-Publication Data
Baker, Keith, 1953–
Sometimes/Keith Baker.
p.   cm.
"Green Light Readers."
Summary: The things that a child feels are different from time to time, but they are all OK.
ISBN 0-15-202002-0
[1. Emotions—Fiction.   2. Senses and sensation—Fiction.   3. Self-acceptance—Fiction.]
I. Title.
PZ7.B17427So 1999
[E]—dc21   98-15561

A C E F D B

The illustrations in this book were done in acrylic paint on illustration board.
The display type was set in Sitcom.
The text type was set in Minion.
Color separations by Bright Arts Ltd., Hong Kong
Printed by South China Printing Company, Ltd., Hong Kong
This book was printed on 140-gsm matte art paper.
Production supervision by Stanley Redfern and Ginger Boyer
Designed by Barry Age